Tangerines
and Tea

My Grandparents and Me

written by ONA GRITZ

illustrated by YUMI HEO

Harry N. Abrams, Inc., Publishers

For Ethan, my boy with the bubbly laugh. —O.G.
For my grandparents. —Y.H.

Artist's Note

When I get a manuscript, I picture myself in the story somewhere as a little bird peeping in the scenes. My imagination begins to wander. Then I ask myself, what would I like to see in this picture? What images would please me? What images would bring a grin to my face?

I do very rough sketches, usually just main images. When I start a final piece, I begin to draw with pencil, adding floating elements in the background spontaneously. Then I spray the drawing with workable fixative and begin to paint with oil. Sometimes I leave my mistakes. Unpainted, smudged pencil lines create a sort of underpainting on my picture. It also allows me not to be afraid, not to worry about being perfect. It gives me a sense of freedom. I hope it will give children the courage to draw and I want them to think it is OK if they make a mistake.

—Y.H.

Design by Angela Carlino
Production Manager: Jonathan Lopes

Library of Congress Cataloging-in-Publication Data

Gritz, Ona.
  Tangerines and tea, my grandparents and me : an ABC book / Ona Gritz ; illustrated by Yumi Heo.
    p. cm.
  Summary: Presents the letters of the alphabet using alliterative rhymes, from "apples to share in the crisp autumn air" to "zithers and guitars beneath zillions of stars."
  ISBN 0-8109-5871-6
  [1. Alphabet. 2. Stories in rhyme.] I. Heo, Yumi, ill. II. Title.

PZ8.3.G893Ta 2005
[E]—dc22
            2004029356

Text copyright © 2005 Ona Gritz
Illustrations © 2005 Yumi Heo

Published in 2005 by Harry N. Abrams, Incorporated, New York. All rights reserved.

Printed and bound in China
10 9 8 7 6 5 4 3 2 1

 Harry N. Abrams, Inc.
100 Fifth Avenue, New York, NY 10011
www.abramsbooks.com

Abrams is a subsidiary of

LA MARTINIÈRE GROUPE

Apples to share in the crisp autumn air,

a boy in a bath with a bubbly laugh,

the corner of the world where the cat lies curled,

dogs that dine from your dish and mine,

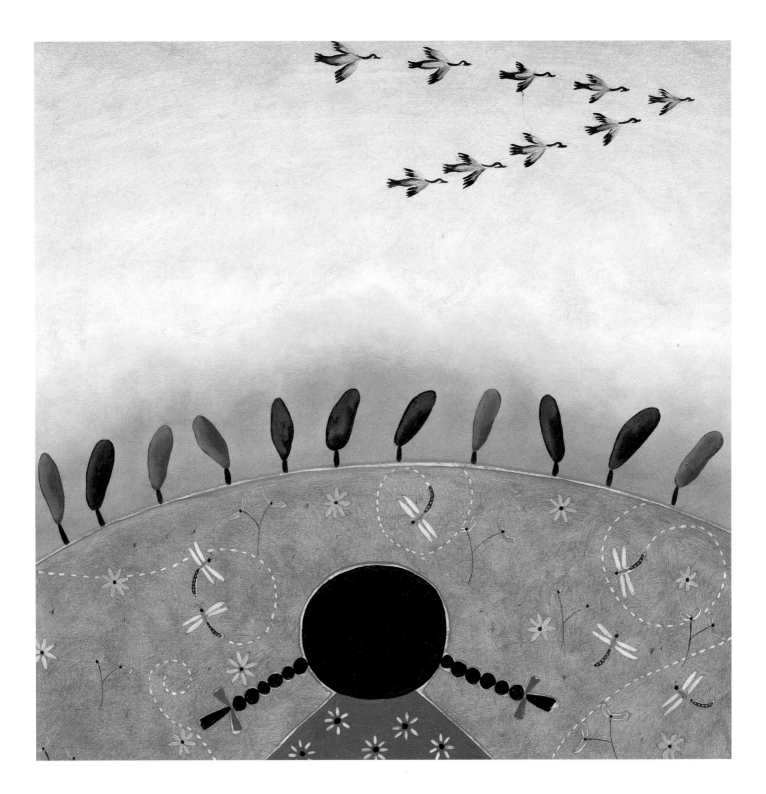

an enchanting display at the end of each day,

a farm where we're free

to pick fruit off a tree,

a good night's rest as our grandparents' guest,

a hunt outside for the best place to hide,

icing to try for those quicker than I,

jewels to explore made with junk from a drawer,

kisses blown through the kitchen phone,

the line of light that I look for at night,

the music we play as we move

through our day,

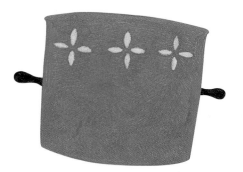

a nap at noon in a noisy room,

an oak tree to climb one limb at a time,

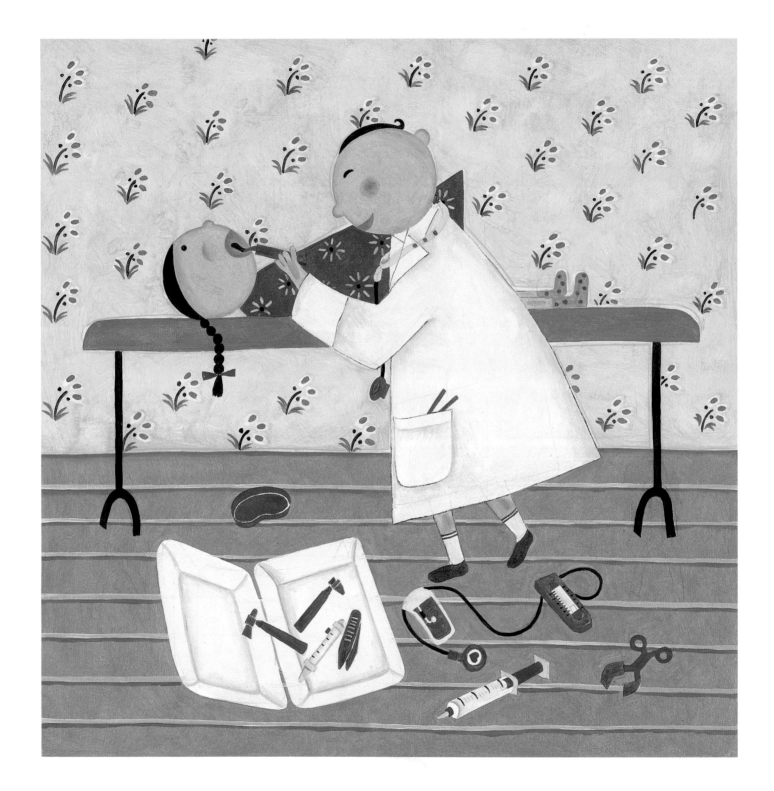

the perfect friend for playing pretend,

the quiet of night with our quilts tucked in tight,

relaxing times reading nursery rhymes,

the songs we sing while we sit on the swing,

tangerines and tea at

the table with me,

the umbrella I'm under when I hear the thunder,

a vivid dream of vanilla ice cream,

a warm wool beret on a wintery day,

X and O—extra kisses to go,

a yard in bloom outside

your room,

and zithers and guitars beneath zillions of stars.